SCOOBY-DOO'S

GUIDE TO LIFE
Just Say "Ruh-roh!"

by Laura Dower

SCHOLASTIC INC.
New York Toronto London Auckland Sydney
Mexico City New Delhi Hong Kong

FOR MY OWN SCOOBY
(YOU KNOW WHO YOU ARE)

ISBN 0-590-63109-8

12 11 10   0 1 2 3 4/0

Interior book design by Louise Bova

Printed in the U.S.A.
First Scholastic printing, February 1999

Dogs, guys, and ghouls everywhere are already talking
about SCOOBY-DOO's *GUIDE* TO LIFE
Critics give it a "Ruh-roh" rousing four dog bones!

"It's a bark-tacular dog tale. If only I'd had Scoobert's guide to
surviving life when I was a young TV pup-start! I could
have rescued even more kids."
— Lassie

"Ruhruhruhruhruhruhruhruhoooooooooooooo!"
— Dino

"Crime fighters must consult this book. Every dog
needs a copy in his or her doghouse."
— Underdog

"Om. Om. Scooby-mmmmmmm."
— The Dalai Llama

"Chickenhearted? Not this dog! Every superhero has his kryp-
tonite. Most of us just don't have anything on Scooby-Doo."
— Superman

"A good slime for everyone — even ghosts!"
— The Swamp Thing

"Paws up, Scooby!"
— Buddy Clinton (the President's pup)

ALREADY APPEARING ON THE *NEW BARK TIMES*
BEST-SELLER LIST!

Greetings From Scooby-Doo

Someone said, "Scooby Snack"! Was it you? Rwoww rwoww rooo! I'm Scooby-Doooooo!

Rello! I was born seven years ago on Knittingham Puppy Farm. My Mommy-Doo and Daddy-Doo named me Scoobert, but I don't like that name much. I'd like it better if you called me Scooby-Doo. That's what my friends call me. And we're friends, right? Zoinks! I rope ro!

I'm a Great Dane and I live in the doghouse behind my friend Shaggy's house. Shaggy and I hang out together and solve mysteries with the rest of the people posse. That's Daphne, Fred, and Velma.

Rahr roo ready to reet them all?

Rooowf! This is a genuine first paw-son account of my life, family, and friends! Believe it or not, I'm going to reveal Scooby's secrets of derring-doo and how to capture bad guys, ghouls, and ghosts. I'm ready to tell you how I walk, talk, and think — so you can be just like me! I'm ready to reveal my top ten mysterious disguises! I'm even ready to share the ultimate secret: the super-duper, hush-hush Scooby Snack recipe! Shhhhhh! As Shaggy says — like, wow, there's a lot to say. Ree-hee-hee.

Welcome to *Scooby-Doo's Guide to Life*. Here's your first tip to be hip: Don't sweat the pup stuff. Rit's reasy to be just like Rooby, right?

SCOOBY'S DOGGY DISH

(Or, What's in My Book)

Chapter 1

THE SCOOBY-DOO FAMILY TREE

Meet the Gang at Mystery, Inc.!

How I Went From Scaredy-cat to Derring Dog

Once upon a time a little puppy (that's me) was born on a little puppy farm. Knittingham Puppy Farm, to be exact. And I was scared of my own little shadow. One look and you'd have thought I was destined for the chicken coop. But not me! This pup grew up . . . and despite my kitty-cat, chickenhearted ways, I learned to be brave and to crack capers of all kinds. In time, I was the derringest dog in the kennel!

How'd it happen?

Don't let my doofy Dane look fool you. Behind this vacant, quaking stare — if I do say so myself — is a mind of mystery-solving genius. Eyebrows twitched, mouth turned up in a sly snicker, paws pointed in the direction of danger, I have tracked down the most menacing of monsters, ghouls, and creeps. No fooling. Ree-hee-hee.

But if I wasn't born to be brave, where do I, the astonishing Scoobert, get my crime-solving savvy?

Is there such a thing as a crime-solving gene? Was my passion for peril inspired by my friends?

Sort of. Check out my tribe on the next few pages.

Meet My People Posse

I get a lot of my talent and smarts and courage from . . . my friends. Yeah, yeah, Scooby-Doo's friends! Let's see . . .

Shaggy: The Original Shaggadelic Scaremeister

I believe that every doggy has his human twin. And mine? Of course he's Shaggy Rogers, the numero uno bestest friend in the whole wide world. Shaggy was born Norville, can you dig that? But Shaggy is a much better name for this skinny dude with the scraggly hair, straggly beard, and shaggarific outfits.

Does anyone have a Scooby Snack? I'm only in chapter one and I am already starving!

7

Zoinks! A floating haunted bone!

Bone? Slurp! Chomp! Gulp!

I guess *haunted* bones are one thing that you're not scared of . . .

Nope! Ree-hee-hee! Scooby-Dooby-Doo!

To me, Shag is the King of Cool — and I'm his doggy Duke! Shaggy and me are, like, closer than close. Actually, I sound a lot like him right now. Like, wow. Ree-hee!

Just like me, Shaggy is scared of his own shadow. (He's scared of his own *squeaking shoes*, for goodness sake!) But we will solve any mystery with the rest of the people posse . . . just so we can chow down afterward! That's where we are absolutely identical and totally twinlike — I'll chase a crook or a creep as long as I can cut a path through the nearest *kitchen*! We live for snacking.

Rat's right! Shaggy and I are the top dogs in our sleuthing agency, Mystery, Inc.

Fred: The Fearless Leader

Of course, I get my singular ghost-tracking skills from other members of the people posse, too! I *ree-lee, ree-lee* admire Fred Jones, the debonair detective of the bunch. He's the all-American blond leader of our pack, the hunk behind the wheel of the Mystery Machine, and the super-duper inventor of secret gadgets to catch our vicious villains.

Fred *always* walks in front of the group.

Fred *always* is the first one to say, "Okay, gang, let's split up."

Fred *always* is the boss.

Ractually, the only thing I don't like about Fred is when he wants me to get the *ghost*'s attention. No matter where we are, no matter what we are doing, Fred always chooses *me* to sneak into that dark cave or crawl down some spooky corridor! Me! Sometimes he asks me to do stuff that gives me the super-creeps. Jeeps!

Even though I don't always like what he asks me to do, I *ree-lee, ree-lee* want to be a leader like Fred someday. Rup!

I think we've stumbled onto some kind of a kookie mystery here!

Daphne: The Don't-Know-Where-to-Go-Next Girl

Daphne Blake is the babe of the group. She's got an eye for mystery and a flair for fashion. Even if she always wears the same purple dress, she's a fashion plate. I think she's cuter than cute.

Thanks to Daphne's millionaire dad, Mystery, Inc. can afford to travel around in the luxurious Mystery Machine, use transmitters and other mechanical doodads, and (I thank my lucky dog stars just to think about it) buy oodles and oodles of deee-licious Scooby Snacks!

I've learned a lot about chasing spooks from hanging around with Daphne. She's the member of our group voted "most likely to be hunted down by an evil spirit." If she has the choice of opening one of three mystery doors, Daphne will definitely choose the one with the black phantom lurking behind it. I remember to keep on my paws when I'm hanging around with Daph!

Four tunnels . . . which one should we take?

Velma: Brainiac Girl

Last but never least, there is Velma Dinkley. She's the real brains of our outfit. With her thick-framed but always-in-style black glasses, freckled face, and orange turtleneck, this smarty-pants detective knows how to figure out all the scientific and logical solutions to our mysteries. She sounds a lot like a dictionary and she's always, *always* right, no matter how much Fred wishes *he* were Mr. Smart.

> Unless my glasses deceive me, we've just found the first clue!

As Shaggy would say, "Like, Velma gets the stuff no one else gets."

Velma's also the one who started the whole "Will you chase the ghost for a Scooby Snack?" thing, although Fred probably wishes he could take credit for that, too. But I know the truth. Velma was the first one to think up food bribes to get me geared up for our very first ghost hunt.

Thanks to Velma, I started stalking things that go bump in the night. Ruh-roh! Scooby-Dooby-Doooo!

Chapter 2

WALK THE SCOOBY WALK

How to Step into Scooby's Paws!

There Isn't a Single Secret to Solving Mysteries

Nope! There isn't a *single* secret to solving 'em — there are a jillion!

You don't believe me? Ruh-roh! You have a LOT to learn before you achieve super Scoobster sleuthing status.

But fear not! This chapter will teach you one of my best secrets: mastering the 'Doo's disguises. After all, if you want to be a daring pooch, the first priority must be lookin' doggone good. With just one snap of your paw, you can walk my walk — and soon you'll be cracking mystery cases in your spare time.

The Big Scooby Disguise: BEFORE

You may think I spend hours on my doggy do, but I don't fuss with my hair at all. Take a look at me — no frills. On page 14 is how I look on an ordinary day — *before* I set out to solve a mystery. Daphne told me once that I was the cutest pooch in Coolsville. Rowff! You should try the all-natural look, too. . . . It's good 2-B-U!

Walk the Fake Walk? Who, Me?

Rulp! It's true . . . it's all true. Even though I like to be myself, I have often tried to fake being sick to get out of solving mysteries. It's not something I'm ree-lee, ree-lee proud of, but I can't help it. I confess, I'm a Not-So-Great Dane sometimes. Like, when I get scared of the dark or even scared of the light, I think up the bestest excuses I can think up. Let's see. . . .

First, I make my paws go limp. It works great. I get lots of sympathy, especially from Daphne.

Next, I let my ears and eyes droop . . . and drag . . .

Finally, I whimper really loudly. You should hear me.

At this point in the fake, however, Shaggy or Fred has usually caught on to my not-really-sick trick. I don't know how they do it every time, but they do. And then — if you can believe this — they'll trick me right back! Usually, Fred will pull me aside and say, "I know you're feeling bad, Scoob, but would you chase that ghoul for a Scooby Snack?"

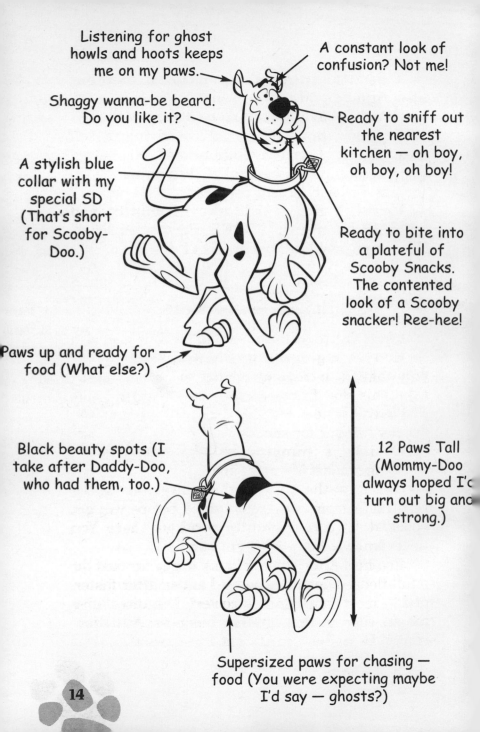

Listening for ghost howls and hoots keeps me on my paws.

A constant look of confusion? Not me!

Shaggy wanna-be beard. Do you like it?

Ready to sniff out the nearest kitchen — oh boy, oh boy, oh boy!

A stylish blue collar with my special SD (That's short for Scooby-Doo.)

Ready to bite into a plateful of Scooby Snacks. The contented look of a Scooby snacker! Ree-hee!

Paws up and ready for — food (What else?)

Black beauty spots (I take after Daddy-Doo, who had them, too.)

12 Paws Tall (Mommy-Doo always hoped I'd turn out big and strong.)

Supersized paws for chasing — food (You were expecting maybe I'd say — ghosts?)

I usually think about it for a moment and sigh.

"Would you do it for TWO Scooby Snacks?"

My ears perk up. Drat! I'm giving myself away. Quick! I sneeze "Rahhhchoo!" Maybe my instant cold in the noze will fool them all.

"For THREE Scooby Snacks?"

I cave. I give in right away! I undroop and jump up, slurping. THREE Scooby Snacks?! There's no way I'm turning THAT down! I'm only a chowhound, after all.

Time to Get to Work

Once Mystery, Inc. needs to solve a puzzle, I need to get in gear — literally. And it only takes one costume change to take this dog from scared — to prepared! When I dress up, my hunger for snacks turns into a hunger for catching crooks! My paws are quicker than the eye — and my disguises mystify! Take it from me — get spiffed before you get spooked. It's a cold, ghostly world out there. You never know what you might run into.

Ree-hee! After trading in my doggy fur coat for a full-fledged detective getup, I am smarter, faster, and — most important — cooler! Disguises give me an edge in this mystery business. Attention, creeps! Be-be-beware of what I w-w-wear!

The Big Scoony Disguise: AFTER

Roowrooo! Here are TEN different ways I dress for ghoul-snagging success!

1. The Cape. *The coolest cover-up, the simple cape will keep you covered from rain, snow, sleet, hail — and ghosts. You can be a king, a count, or a superdog. Or, if all else fails, you can curl up in a corner and hide. Also used as capes: sheets, blankets, and shower curtains — good to use as a ghost disguise when pretending to scare other ghosts. You can even scare your friends. Sometimes I hide under a blanket in the back of the Mystery Machine — and shock the Shagster! Ree-hee!*

2. The Crown. *The costume clincher. Who would run from a regal beagle or a crowned hound? A Great Dane like me wearing a crown has ruler written all over him . . . ruler of ghouls! Yeeeeooow! Sometimes Daphne helps me cover my crown in different jewels and gems for the raja look if ghost hunting in India or other exotic places.*

3. The Wig. *The ultimate in witch wear. Pointed hat optional. The perfect cover-up, a furry wig can also transform even the homliest hound into a beautiful werewolf. Purple and green hair is prefurred. Bleeee-hee!*

4. The Loincloth. *The caveman look is, like, totally in for disguises. This one is Shaggy's favorite. He says, "Like, why not goof on a ghost! Make him think he's scared you out of your own skin, man. Yuk! Yuk!" Warning: Make sure any loincloth is tightly attached for extra-long chases. I never like to get caught with my fur flying free.*

5. The Eyepatch. *Blimey! Ghosts, monsters, and PIRATES, ahoy! This simple black patch deceives the monster I'm chasing every time! Plus, it's also good for fooling friends like Fred during card games and other tricky moments when you need just the right look. A favorite for seafaring ghost hunts, the eye patch is dangerous when chasing ghouls down dark corridors. I wear my patch with my own paper pirate hat.*

6. The Large Globe Helmet with Strange Tubes and Air Tanks. *Astronaut? Scoob-a diver? Outer space creep? No one will know what's what or who's who when you're caught* up in this getup. I don't even know what it is, but Velma says it's "satisfactorily submergible" — whatever that means — and Daphne agrees it's groovy! Shaggy says it's the best outfit of all because it's so, like, weird. And I guess if I were a ghoul in a chase, I'd run from weird space aliens, too. Wouldn't you?

7. **The Mask.** *Any kind of mask will do as long as there's a place for me to scream back to ghosts, "Boooooooby-Dooby-Doo!" When wearing someone else's creepy face, the acting bug really bites me! I've been a zombie, an ancient warlord, a wolfman, and many more. Like, it's so creeptacular!*

8. **Barrel.** *A seemingly simple disguise, the common wooden barrel is a last resort for ghoul-trackers like me. Jump in and hide. Pop out when they run back. It's that simple. Surprise is on my side.*

9. **Wax Museum.** *No, this isn't a specific disguise as in costume, but it is a disguise as in pose. Here's how it works: When chasing monsters, I usually end up running into a dark and super-spooky tunnel, through a fun house, and inside a mysterious wax museum. Aha! That's where my disguise becomes ultraclear. I*

jump onto one of the exhibits and assume a strange, Scooby-arms-in-the-air pose. The ghosts almost never recognize me — yulp! — I hope.

10. **Human.** *When all else fails, I try the most unassuming of all disguises, the human costume. Just when the ghoul thinks it knows how many people to scare — there's one more . . . me! . . . in a blond wig or maybe a T-shirt or maybe just a suit and tie. And then what is that ghoul supposed to do? Chances are, it'll be so confused, it'll let me get away. . . .*

DON'T TRY THIS AT HOME, KIDS!

The Sturgeon General has determined that costumed disguises like these are to be used only by trained professional ghost trackers like Scooby-Doo, his buddy Shaggy, and other select members of the people posse. If you or someone you know happens to be testing out the eye patch, mask, or curly wig, please make sure you're ready to come face-to-face with the same dangerous monsters haunting Mystery, Inc. Wearing Scooby's strange disguises has been known to cause *mysterious* side effects.

19

Chapter 3

TALK THE SCOOBY TALK

How to Make Hound Sounds!

Say What?!!

Are you all ears? I've got just the right thing for you to say when you're making tracks for the next ghost stop! Sound good so far?

Pick out which look of mine you like the most from the chart on pages 22-23 — is it the "bewildered, googly-eyed" look or perhaps the "dumbfounded, you-can't-be-serious" look? Next to each one, you'll find one of my Scooby-isms listed — along with an explanation of what I ree-lee mean when I make that face and talk the Scooby talk. Zoinks!

Even More Ways to Talk the Talk

In addition to using my favorite expressions, both spoken and unspoken, there are s'more ways to start talking like me. Scooby Speak is as easy as 1-2-3!

1. Add an "R" sound to the beginning of all words. So "uh-oh" would be "ruh-roh!"
2. Add a few extra syllables to your words. Why keep your words so short? Which would you

pick: "Delicious" or "Deeeee-licious?" I vote for the second one! Ruch retter, right?

3. If you exclaim something and shout it out . . . say it TWICE! Like, when I say "Scooby Snack?" I follow it up with a quick, higher-pitched, "Scooby Snack!" You try it.

Scooby Speak isn't the only lingo spoken in Coolsville. Everyone in the gang has his or her own quirky quips! Wanna rap like Shaggy or sound as smart as Velma? You betcha! But don't ask me how to do it — ask THEM! By special invitation, I now present the members of Mystery, Inc. with their own tips on talking their kind of talk.

Shaggy Rogers: Like, He's a Cool Speaker. Dig It?

Like, wow, I sure do have, like, the grooviest gift for gab. Shagster here, and, like, I know how to talk cooler than cool and you can, too! Listen to this, man:

1. Like, obviously you have to, like, add the word *like* to the beginning of everything you say. Like, of course.

2. Stutter away, my friends! Like, I've never seen a chatterbox ghost hunter like me. You can tell when I'm afraid by the way I sp-sp-speak!

LOOK	WHAT I SAY	WHAT I MEAN
a.	Ruh-roh!	Ruh-roh. . . . What do you think? [Uh-oh.]
b.	Wha' zat?	*Did you hear a wrapper open?*
c.	(silence)	Watch how I get me an extra Scooby Snack.
d.	Yip! Yip! Yip!	Did someone say Scooby Snack?
e.	Ree-hee!	I'm so silly.
f.	Sssssluuuurp!	*All this detecting makes me hungry.*
g.	Ruf!	I'm a super sleuth!

LOOK	WHAT I SAY	WHAT I MEAN
h.	Sor-ree	Ooooh! I am so embarrassed!
i.	(whistle noise)	Shaggy, over here! I found the buffet!
j.	Rahhhrrr!	Hey, you! Hands off my Scooby Snack!
k.	Gullllp	Who, me? You think I ate that Scooby Snack?
l.	Yiii! Yiii!	Chowhound coming through!
m.	*Phooof!*	*Made it home for dinner!*
n.	Scooby-Dooby-Doo!	Scooby-Dooby-Doo!

Here are so-so-some of my f-f-favorite all-time Shaggy stutters:

- Wh-wh-what wa-wa-wax pha-phantom!
- H-h-hang on, S-S-Scoob!
- I'm n-n-n-nervous enough!
- Wh-wh-wh-what's *that?*
- Po-po-pogo sti-sti-stick? This is a ja-ja-jack hammer!

3. Talk about *food,* man! I'm hungry for the right words all the time — and if you're talking double-fudge sundaes with pickles on top, you're talking my language! Yuk! Yuk!

4. Like, start words with the same letter, man. Don't say "wacky ghost" when you can say "gooney ghost!" It sounds so much cooler that way!

5. Rhyme like it's goin' out-a-style, man. Make "scary" into "hairy scary" and turn "Tiki" into "freaky Tiki!"

6. Sing out loud, groovy one! A little hum-dee-dum will pass the time while you're waiting for ghosts to appear.

7. Throw a little yodel in your speak once in a while. Don't say, "I am doomed." That's so, like, boooor-ing! Say it out loud like you're falling off a cliff: "I'm doooooooooomed!"

8. Add "-est" to everything you say. I do it so everything I'm talking

about sounds like it's the bestest thing that ever was. Don't say "cool," say "coolest." Don't say "ghoul," say "ghoulest." Don't say "Shaggy," say "Shaggiest!" Yuk! Yuk!

Fred Jones Speaks His Mind

Jumpin' jelly beans! Being a detective sure is hard work. Do you think you're up for it? This whole mystery thing can be pretty puzzling.

So, you want to be more like me, huh? Well, that's a tall order to fill. I'm a unique kind of guy. But I can give you a few pointers about how you can be brilliant, take-charge, and totally in control like me. Now, here's a plan. Follow my instructions carefully.

1. First, get the right look. I take great care in the way I present myself. Scooby doesn't call me the head honcho for nothing. For instance, you can't even begin to think about tracking a monster unless you're wearing a scarf like mine. I know this really has nothing to do with talking, but somehow I believe the right outfit makes me say the right things.

2. Second, take control of each situation with an assertive statement. I start off most thoughts with, "Hey, gang, listen to me." It's important to get everyone's attention right off the bat.

3. Third, delegate. Are there ghosts to be found? Make sure everyone knows what to do, as in, "You go, Scoob!" As the leader, I can't let myself get caught up in the details. My job is to keep order. As you know, the three most important words in Fred-speak are "let's split up." I say where we go and who goes where.

4. Lastly, if you want to truly be like me, you need to be present at the moment of truth. Just as the creeps are dashing away, step in and say, "You're not going anywhere!" And no matter what else happens, always be there when the ghoul is revealed. In Fred-speak, you announce that by saying, "Now . . . Mr. _____, it's time to find out who you *really are!*" It works like a charm.

5. Act surprised at all times, especially when the criminals fix their evil stare on you and sputter, "If it weren't for those meddling kids!" They always say that. You'll get used to it.

Daphne Blake Blanks Out

Jeepers! You wanna know what I say and how I say it? Well, to start, I agree with Fred. Looking good helps me feel and say the right things. What you wear makes a statement all its own. For sure! Like my hair. But I have to dress practically, too. Comfortable yet stylish shoes are a super-sleuthing must.

I'm a real detective, you know. Wow! I wanna be a mystery writer and all that. Yeesh!

But I'm getting off the subject at hand. So . . . you want to talk . . . like *me*?

All I can say is that you need to use groovy words like, "This ghost ship really gives me the chills," or "Golly, this place sure is creepy," or even "This sure is strange-o!"

Oh! And don't forget if ya wanna be like me that you'll be sorta danger-prone, too, so you should practice all kinds of shouts and screams to let everyone know where the ghost is hiding. "Eeeeek!" is good. So is "Yiiiiiikes!" Whatever you like best I guess. Just remember: You're not really *scared*, you're just trying to make the bad ghouls think you are. Pretty tricky, right?

The Dinkley Formula:
Talk Smart With Velma

According to my guidebook, the proper way to speak like me, Velma Dinkley, is to talk with big, important words. And you don't even have to know what they mean or anything like that. I mean, it helps to know, but sounding smart is what matters.

Simplified, all you need to do is add letters to every word you say and create bigger, more authoritative words. My research tells me that people will be amazed! You can impress your friends at school and ace your language tests. Tell 'em Velma taught you how to do it! Soon everyone will be talking like me.

Even smart people have their favorite expressions. If you want to sound like me, then it's logical to memorize the following key phrases:

- Jinkies!
- Cool it!
- Hold on to your hula hoops!
- Be careful!
- Unless my glasses deceive me . . .

When you "talk Velma," you need to STAY CURIOUS. To begin with, I wear investigating glasses so I always strike that curious pose. And the question mark is my favorite kind of punctuation! Even more important, I start every sentence with a thoughtful, "Hmmmmmmm?" That's me!

In closing, let me add that I always try to have the answers. So if you're responding like Velma and someone asks you a question, you need to know everything. Of course, this means that in order to *really* talk like me, you need to study every obscure dictionary and encyclopedia available in the library. That's how I do it.

Jinkies! How else could I possibly know what I know about Phospherum Pirifera, a strange phosphorescent seaweed on ghost ships? Or how can I map the location of ancient Druid ruins in foreign countries? Go figure! I'm Velma Dinkley! Good luck being me!

Chapter 4

THINK THE SCOOBY THINK

Words of Wisdom and 45 Runny Rooby Riddles

Do What You Love, The Scooby Snacks Will Follow

Yipes . . . and double Yipes! What do I say to people who ask me what they should do with their lives? I guess there are three pieces of advice I would give any human or dog:

1. Be yourself — big paws and all.

2. Do what you love to do and don't worry about it.

3. Follow your heart and be good to your friends.

Chickenhearted Soup for the Soul

Just a few more nuggets of wisdom from Scooby the wise for you to recite to yourself before the big test or the big game:
- Why chase creeps and zombies all day long? Because they're there!

- The road to happiness is paved with Scooby Snacks.
- Stop and smell the roses — and whatever else is cooking.
- Anything worth doing is worth doing the Scooby way.

1. Friends and family lend a hand when you're in trouble.
   Hey — remember when Velma set a trap and saved me and Shaggy from the monster?

2. Friends and family cheer you up when you're sad or afraid.
   Hey — remember when I gave Shaggy a big slurp of a kiss when he was scared?

3. Friends and family keep in touch even across far distances.
   Hey — remember when we went to visit Daphne's aunt and uncle at the beach?

4. Friends and family listen when you talk.
   Hey — why do you think I repeat almost everything Shaggy says? Because I'm listening so good!

5. Friends and family don't mind getting close to one another.
   Hey — remember when Shaggy and I went to the parade piled up together?

Forty-five ree-diculous riddles? Oh boy, oh boy, oh boy! Now that you can walk the walk and talk the talk, one more way to be like me is to **think my think**! Huh? Wha' zat? Simple: Train your human brain to get as silly as a petrified pooch brain!

WARNING! The following riddles may cause laugh attacks and make the riddler more Scooby-like! Double zoinks!

Test these out on your teachers, friends, parents, Little League coach, bus driver, cafeteria lady — anyone who'll listen to you!

Why did Scooby-Doo get fat?

Because he asked for too many second yelpings!

What did Scooby answer when the dentist asked him what kind of filling he wanted?

"Rhocolate."

Why did Shaggy keep running around his bed?

Like, because he wanted to catch some ZZZZZ's.

Why does Shaggy only draw circles?

Because he's too cool, dude. He doesn't like squares!

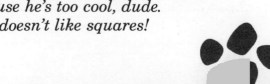

Why did Daphne and Fred take the ghost they caught to the doctor?

They were worried because it wasn't in very good spirits.

Why isn't Velma feeling well?

Because she has a pair of gloves on her hands!

What kind of tea can help Scooby to feel brave?

Safe-ty.

What did Shaggy do when Scooby tried to swallow a book?

He took the words right out of his mouth!

Why did Scooby-Doo fail his ghost test?

He made too many boo-boos!

What kind of cheese does Shaggy like to eat on his hero sandwiches?

Muenster.

What game did Scooby-Doo play with the Abominable Snowman?

Freeze tag.

Why did Scooby and the rest of the people posse go on safari?

They wanted to do some big-game haunting.

Shaggy: Hey, Scoob, what should you say to a giant, hungry monster?

Scooby: Nothing! Just run away!

Velma: Did you hear about the party at the cemetery last night?

Daphne: I heard the place was dead.

If Scooby-Doo, Shaggy, Daphne, Fred, and Velma were all trying to fit under one umbrella, how come none of them got wet?

Jinkies! Because it wasn't raining.

What fruit snack does Dracula like to ask for?

Neck-tarines.

And what does Dracula say when Scooby and Shaggy give him that snack?

Fangs very much.

What do you get when you cross Scooby-Doo and a chicken?

Pooched eggs!

How do the people posse like their eggs cooked?

Terri-fried!

What kind of snacks do sea monsters like to nosh on?

Fish and ships.

What do Scooby and Shaggy like to eat on October 31?

Halloweenies!

Why did Scooby-Doo cross the road?

Because the chicken was on vacation.

What happened to the TNT Monster when Fred found it in the refrigerator?

It blew its cool.

What do Scooby and a train have in common?

They both chew, chew, chew.

How does Shaggy make a super-duper milk shake?

He sneaks up behind it and yells, "Boo!"

What was Mommy-Doo's favorite saying?

A stitch in time saves canine!

Why did Shaggy go into the kitchen?

To scare up some food!

What does Scooby call the
top of the Mystery Machine?

The woof!

Fred: Do you know how long
monsters should be fed?

Daphne: The same as
short monsters!

What white, fluffy food does Scooby-Doo like to
eat at the movies?

Pupcorn!

Shaggy: Like, wow, guys, we're
already outa ghoulash?

Velma: That's stew bad!

What kinds of food does the gang eat in the
Mystery Machine?

Fast *food*!

How did Velma know how to
capture the Mountain Monster?

She returned to the scene of the climb!

Why does Shaggy call the Mystery Machine the Invisible Van?

Because, like wow, it's out-a-sight!

How did the gang know that the Mystery Machine was in pain?

Because its brakes kept screeching!

What do Daphne and Velma discuss when they're alone?

Just ghoul talk!

Shaggy: Like, when is the best time to have lunch?

Scooby: Rafter reakfast!

Fred asked Scooby to watch the Mystery Machine. Why did Scooby get a ticket?

Because he was double-barked!

What do hungry ghost hunters do between snacks?

They burp!

Fred: Hey, Shaggy, here's a pie! Should I cut it into six slices?

Shaggy: Like, no way, man, I couldn't eat that much. Cut it into **four** pieces!

What is the best thing that
Chef Shaggy put into the pie?

His teeth!

Why doesn't the Sea Beast have
time to stop and chat?

He's swamped right now.

Why didn't Velma see the ghost?

She dropped her spook-tacles!

What did Shaggy and Scooby scream to the
gang while they were chasing ghosts?

Run! Run! The ghost is clear!

What song did Shaggy and
Scooby sing for the Mummy?

A wrap song.

Knock, knock.

Who's there?

Scooby.

Scooby who?

Scooby-Dooby-Doooo!

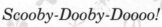

Chapter 5

SCOOBY SNACK TIME

Original Recipes from Scooby and the Rest of the Gang!

Rrrrrrooof! Presenting the grooviest collection of recipes from the Scooby Snack Factory! Now you can make my favorite snacks — IF you can *really* stomach th' stuff!

From pizza pockets to mile-high sandwiches to super sweets, you can't enjoy the Scooby way of life without LOTS of food! Some of these groovy recipes do not require cooking — or eating, for that matter — but have fun with them anyway! For the REAL recipes, don't forget to ask your own Mommy-Doo or Daddy-Doo for help if you're working in the kitchen. Rahhhroooo!

RECIPES JUST FOR FUN

Ruh-roh, Don't Try These at Home!

Shaggy's Super-Duper Hero Sandwich

As you know, the Shagster likes to make, like, totally shaggadelic food constructions. His tallest sandwich (*which I stole and ate for myself . . . ree-hee!*) was measured at one foot — high! This is one recipe that might be a little too gross for you. Rulp!

Ingredients:

★ lettuce, tomatoes, pickles, and peanut butter
★ large loaf of Italian or French bread
★ 3 chocolate bars (nuts optional)
★ mayonnaise, ketchup, chocolate sauce, hot sauce

Do This:

1. Slice bread into two long pieces.
2. Pile on the food and sauces.
3. Snarf sandwich in less than five bites, just like Shaggy.
4. Lick lips and say, "Mmmmmmm. Like, wow, gimme another one!"

Now, let's hit the sack.

First, I'm gonna hit the ol' lunch sack! With a Shaggy Super Sandwich!

Daphne's Trapdoor Dip

I can't believe it sometimes when Daphne gets all mixed up and picks the wrong door or window . . . and we end up running for our lives! This is a recipe that Shaggy and I made up in Daphne's honor. We think she should use this as a recipe for NOT getting caught by surprise by a three-eyed monster behind a trapdoor! Fill a bucket with this stuff and hurl it at the nearest ghoul. Guaranteed to soak at least one villain.

Ingredients:

★ 5 cups flour
★ 6 cups soda water
★ 1 cup of wilted snakeskin
★ 500 ants, legs removed
★ 4 tablespoons of ghost sweat
★ a fistful of wolf hair
★ 1 tube of glue
★ green food coloring
★ eye of newt
★ 12 cups of wet mud

Do This:

★ Mix all the stuff together — except the ghost sweat.
★ Toss the mix into the air and sing a nursery rhyme while standing on your head. Add the ghost sweat very carefully.
★ Count to one million.

* Refrigerate mix for one month.
* Attack a creep with it.
* Celebrate your ghost-busting success.

RECIPES FOR REAL

Ruh-roh, Ask a Grown-up for Help!

Rysterious Rango Smoothie

(er . . . that's Mysterious Mango in non-Scoob speak)

I'll wait here and guard this delicious bowl of fruit.

Guard it?

Sure . . . what safer place than in my stomach? Chomp!

RUH-ROH!
REAL RECIPE
ASK YOUR PARENTS FOR HELP

Shaggy and I loooooove frozen drinks. Well, we really loooooove CHOCOLATE frozen drinks, but Daphne warned us that we should try to think a little healthier — so we turned our chocolate sm-mm-mmooth milk shake into a fruit-tastic smoothie. Gimme! Gimme!

41

Hey, Scoob, look! Buffet table at three o'clock!

I'm with you!

Ingredients:

★ 1 mango
★ 2 cups vanilla ice cream

Do This:

1. Slice the mango.
2. Put mango and ice cream into a blender.
3. Blend and gulp.

Special Note: *If you want, you can substitute other fruits for the mango. Try strawberries or a banana. Oranges will not work. Neither will pears. Shaggy tried a tomato once, but that was, like, ree-lee weird. You figure it out. I'm not thirsty now anyway.*

Shaggy's Pep-Pep-Pepper Pizza Wh-Wh-Wheels

Okay, you know how much Shaggy loves to eat. But above every other kind of food in the whole universe, he thinks pizza is just perfect. Yummmm! Me too!

Ingredients:

* ★ 4 English muffins
  (each cut in half)
* ★ 1 cup pizza or spaghetti sauce
* ★ 1 cup grated mozzarella cheese
* ★ 1 cup chopped red and
  green bell peppers

Open the mouth . . .
between th' gums . . .
Look out, stomach . . .
Here it comes!

Do This:

1. Toast the English muffin
   halves (eight in all) in a toaster.
2. Top each with sauce,
   cheese, and peppers.
3. Bake five minutes or
   so in toaster oven.
4. Chow down!

Freddy's Fortune Cookies

Know-it-all Fred dreamed up this "kooky" recipe when we had some downtime after one of our ghost hunts. Here's what makes it so cool: You can fill the cookies with Scooby fortunes like, "You will meet a strange monster at a shipwreck," or "There is nothing to be afraid of," or "Fiddle-dee-dee! Future looks groovy!" Make up your own funky fortunes!

Ingredients:

* ★ 1/4 cup flour
* ★ 2 tablespoons sugar
* ★ 1 tablespoon cornstarch
* ★ pinch of salt

- ★ 2 tablespoons cooking oil
- ★ 1 egg white
- ★ 1 tablespoon water
- ★ vegetable cooking spray

Other Stuff You'll Need:
- ★ 8 strips of paper with your Scooby messages
- ★ medium bowl for mixing
- ★ tablespoon for measuring
- ★ frying pan/skillet
- ★ paper towels
- ★ measuring cup

Do This:
- ★ Combine flour, sugar, cornstarch, and salt in your mixing bowl.
- ★ Add oil and egg white and stir carefully. Get out all the lumps!
- ★ Add water and mix together well.
- ★ Make each cookie separately! Pour one tablespoon of batter onto the frying pan/skillet (that's been sprayed with the vegetable spray).
- ★ Cook for about three minutes until it browns. Turn over. Cook 1 minute.
- ★ Place on paper towel and wipe off extra grease.
- ★ Put paper fortune in the middle and fold cookie together to make fortune cookie shape.
- ★ Cool and start over again until, like, all the "kookies" are done. Cool!

I've Got a Clue! Treasure Cups

Velma is just about the smartest sleuth in town — or in the world, for that matter. So what does this smarty-pants like to snack on? Buried treasure! In the mystery business, we find treasure chests in the most surprising places. Now you can make treasure in your own kitchen. Row-reee!

Ingredients:

* ★ 1 cup blueberries
* ★ 1 cup seedless grapes
* ★ 1 cup sliced strawberries
* ★ 1 cup orange slices
* ★ 1 cup sliced banana
* ★ 1 cup whipped cream
* ★ M&M's and other colored candies
* ★ 8 pieces of gold-foil-wrapped chocolate coins

Other Stuff You'll Need:

* ★ 8 tall clear glasses
* ★ spoon

Do This:

* ★ Place a chocolate coin at the bottom of each glass.
* ★ Layer each different kind of fruit in the glasses.
* ★ Cover with whipped cream and candies.

Scooby and I will head the cleanup committee . . .

Gulp! We will??

Clean up the *food*, that is!

I can already taste those chocolate-covered pickles!

EVEN MORE SCOOBY FOOD FUN!

Zombie Burgers, Anyone?

Remember when we were chased by the Zombies? Like, double yipes! They scared the fur right off me! Shag and I were noshing around the grill and we dreamed up a tribute to those blank-starin' strangers! Decorate your hamburgers or veggie burgers before you eat 'em. Put on pickles for eyes, dots of ketchup or mayonnaise for lips, a lettuce leaf for hair, and so on. Get your revenge when you take a big bite — of zombie head!

Yuck! His stomach must be made of scrap iron!

I can't help it if my first toy was a garbage disposal.

Daphne's Cookie Choker

Darlin' Daph thought of a groovy way for you to make sugar cookies the next time you're mixing and rolling the dough! Wear your dessert on a cookie necklace! Daphne thinks this is great when you're on the go (like we always are in our Mystery Machine). Follow any standard cookie recipe and when it comes time to shape and bake, remember two things: don't make any cookies bigger than 1/2" around, and make circle holes in the center of each one with a toothpick while they're freshly baked and still warm. Once they're done you'll have teeny cookies to string on a necklace!

Yummmm!
Chocolate-Covered Pickles!

So you don't think chocolate-covered pickles sound very good to eat? Boy, oh boy — you don't know what you're missing! Chocolate-covered ANYTHING works for me. Try some of these: chocolate-covered potato chips, chocolate-covered pretzels, even chocolate-covered chocolate! Melt chocolate over low heat and then dip away! Cool for a moment and then dip again. Dip a few times to get the chocolate layered as it hardens.

Oh boy! Oh boy! Oh boy!

The Official, Secret Scooby Snacks Recipe

You have to swear on your cousin's furry paw that you will not reveal the secret "from scratch" recipe for Scooby Snacks to ANYONE except your closest friends!

Ingredients:
- ★ 1/4 cup butter
- ★ 1 cup brown sugar
- ★ 1 egg
- ★ 1 teaspoon vanilla
- ★ 1/2 cup flour
- ★ 1 teaspoon baking powder
- ★ 1/2 teaspoon salt
- ★ 3/4 cup grated coconut

Other Stuff You'll Need:
- ★ mixing bowl
- ★ saucepan
- ★ cookie sheet
- ★ measuring cup
- ★ toothpick

Do This:
- ★ Melt butter in saucepan and stir in sugar until it dissolves.
- ★ Cool and then add egg and vanilla.
- ★ Stir together flour, baking powder, and salt.
- ★ Stir into the butter mixture and then add coconut.
- ★ Drop 1/2" cookies onto sheet and press with fingers into diamond shapes.
- ★ Use the end of a toothpick to press the letters *SD* into each one.
- ★ Bake at 350° for six minutes or until golden brown.
- ★ Serve Scooby Snacks when you catch your next ghost — or sooner. *Don't forget to save some for me! Yum! Yum!*

From Footprints to Trapdoors to Every Other Trick in the Book!

Take a Walk on the Wild Side....

Rrrrrrready to take on the monsters yourself?

Not so fast.

In order to be more like Scooby (that's me), FIRST you need to know how to sniff out danger signs. And remember the main rule of the 'Doo: DON'T get yourself all twisted into a fur ball! Yeah, right. Ree-hee-hee. Shaggy and I are *always* pressing our own panic button.

From the home office in Coolsville, here's my "top ten" list to get your nose in spooky sniffing shape!

YOU KNOW YOU'RE
IN TROUBLE WHEN . . .

1. **You're sleeping and you hear strange snoring . . . *very* strange snoring**. When you shove the person next to you and mumble, "Shaggy, stop it," there's no answer. You open your eyes and . . . WHAM! It's no person snoring, it's a monster — breathing!

2. **You discover a busted phone!** "Hey, this phone is dead. . . . Helllloooo? . . . is anyone there?" Gulp.

3. **Someone's sending smoke signals.** You're chasing a ghost when suddenly a blanket of smoke fills the air and you lose track of the ghoul you had your eye on.

4. **The spotlight's on Y-O-U!** Out of the darkness, you see a light. Oh no! It's a tiki torch! Oh no! It's a lantern! Oh no! It's a *floating* candle . . . and I'm freaked out!

5. **You start hallucinating.** A phantom flies by — and right through a wall!

6. **A duh-head speaks.** Some duh-head says, "Well, I guess we lost them." Of course they show up again ten seconds later.

7. **Another duh-head speaks.** Some other duh-head says, "Do you get the feeling we're not alone?"

8. **Surprise! You're eye to eye with the ghoul.** You're admiring a painting in the hall when suddenly you notice that the eyes in the painting are following you!

9. **Someone interrupts your sleuthing.** You turn your back on a lovely marble statue — all of a sudden it reaches out and taps you on the shoulder!

10. **You decide to step on it.** You step into a giant hole in the grave-yard — and realize that it's ree-lee the footprint of a huge monster lizard. Yeeesh!

Once you've got your doggy derring-doo in gear, you can move on to the "ruff" stuff. Here's a simple Mystery, Inc., five-step formula for catching ghosts that never fails. You try it.

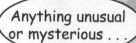

Like, what kind of clues are we looking for?

Anything unusual or mysterious . . .

You mean like the door slamming and locking behind us? Yikes!

Get-Your-Ghost Step I:
Be Observant

Keep those eyes peeled! The best detectives are observant, like our resident smart sleuth, Velma Dinkley. This brainiac knows a clue when she sees one. Velma's always the one to spot the crumpled treasure map or the secret page that's been ripped from a count's diary or a newspaper clipping that's floating in a puddle. In fact, Velma's got the handbook of ghoul-trapping technicalities memorized.

Most important, you can count on Velma to be OBSERVANT enough to identify what a ghoul leaves behind. Forget fingerprints! Velma's always got her eye on . . . footprints!

Hey, look! Footprints!

There's something funny about those footprints!

Footprints! I wonder where they go? Maybe they can lead us to the answer!

Footprints! Let's follow them!

Look at that! The tracks go in different directions!

We'd better find Shaggy and Scooby.... Maybe they've found some clues!

That'll be the day!

Silly ghouls! Ree-hee! Here are just a few of the paw-thetic ways those lead-footed ghosts gave themselves away! Whether slimy, dusty, cracked, invisible, muddy, or rocky . . . Velma *makes* tracks *finding* tracks! As she says, "Hmmmmm. I've got a hunch we're gonna find something here. . . ."

- Quick! Follow that sticky trail of wax footprints up a wall! The Wax Phantom strikes again!

- How on earth can we catch an *invisible* phantom? Hey, wait a minute! Check out that phantom's dirty feet!

- We caught the mysterious Dr. Jekyll from footprints that weren't there! We found the suction cups he used to trick us when he climbed the walls!

- Who else leaves such sludgy tar tracks except for the terrifying Tar Monster!

- Who's afraid of the Big Bad Werewolf's dusty tracks? Not Mystery, Inc.!

- We spotted the glowing ghost footprints underwater! Too bad Captain Cutler's diving suit got covered with that kooky glowing seaweed!

- Look! Over there! Footprints end at the gorge! That can only mean one thing: The Creeper's in the cave! As Daphne would say, "Jeepers! It's the Creeper!"

- What a drip! The extra-large caveman gave himself away with his own melted ice footprints!

Get-Your-Ghost Step II: Be Crafty

Sneak around and you'll snag the spooks! Freddy does his best by setting all sorts of weird traps and tricks to stop those ghosts dead in their tracks. He's stashed secret stuff in the back end of the Mystery Machine so he can pull it out at the scene of the crime — just in time — to catch a thief!

Ruh-roh! If I were a ghoul on the go, I wouldn't want to get tripped up by one of Freddy's CRAFTY contraptions. He's always plotting some kind of undercover operation backed up by the best kind of monster bait!

- *Operation Wax This!* With a wrench and a tub of wax, Fred hooks up a shower sprayer to surprise the real Wax Phantom! When the fake ghoul steps under the shower he'll get a taste of his own medicine when he gets wet — with *wax*!

- *Operation Tricky Tiki!* Fred scrounged around in the back of the Mystery Machine and found his handy-dandy Trick Amusement Park Mirror. Now Fred can hide it in the jungle so when the Witch Doctor faces it, he'll run from his own reflection!

- *Operation Zombie Bomb!* Mixing together a Chinese gong, a couple of Roman candle rockets, and Shaggy's model train set hidden in the back of the Mystery Machine — Freddy can blow the zany Zombie right into the pigeon coop!

- *Operation Slippery Suds!* Get into position down by the yacht marina! Put some liquid soap in a spray container, attach to a fire hose, turn on water, and —

squooosh! — instant suds! Before you know it, the ghost slips on the soap, Fred hoses him into the net, and we all hoist him up, up, and away!

- *Operation Decoy!* While hanging out in your paddleboat, head into the fog bank, and wait for your ghost to be toast! Switch on your handy-dandy tape recorder — which, by the way, has a tape recording of foghorns and ship whistles. Confuse the ghost and jump ship!

Get-Your-Ghost Step III: Watch Your Step

Row-reee! Leave it to Daphne to find her favorite creep. When asked where a villain's vanished, Daphne can sure pick 'em! She's greater than great at finding where horror is hiding! If you show her three doors, she'll scare the spirit out from behind one of them. But there *is* a flip side to this spooky skill. You don't want to ask her to show you the way *away* from danger. She only knows how to find it.

I once read that old castles were loaded with traps!

Oh, Velma! Don't be silly . . . that only happens in movies.

Daphne . . . Daphne!

Wha-wha-what happened?

Daphne fell through the trapdoor.

Where would YOU look for a ghoul? There are plenty of rooms and objects to stake out when you're hunting the haunters of a big ol' house. Just remember: WATCH YOUR STEP!

- **The Twirling Bookcase** *Move the copy of* The Hunchback of Great Dane *and the bookcase suddenly twists around! Do it twice — or three times — in a row, and pretty soon you're booked into a revolving door! Good luck getting off this ride, ghosty!*

- **Escape Lever** *A statue arm, a faucet, a door-knocker, an umbrella. What do those have in common? Escape levers to sneak into walls and floors and get away!*

- **Hidden Staircase** *Push a button and the wall in the hall turns into 39 steps! Going up?*

- **Mysterious Elevator** *That's no painting! That's the control for the secret wall elevator! Going down?*

- **Trapdoor** *One minute you're standing in the library, and the next minute you're falling down, down, down for a crash landing in the basement. And wait! That's no basement . . . that's the hidden chamber of a secret alien tribe! Ree-hee!*

- **Floating Furniture** *Go for the coolest get-away when you hop aboard the speeding sofa or maybe even the flying carpet!*

- **Secret Tunnel** *Drop to your knees, shimmy into the vent, and crawl. Hey, is this some sort of secret passage?*

- **Cellar Slide** *Watch out where you step or you'll end up on a slide ride . . . into a part of the house you never knew existed!*

- **Bat-filled Belfry** *Follow that bat! Climb up, up, up the stairway until you get to the very top — where a bunch of bats would be happy to share their attic with you!*

- **The Dummy Decoy** *Stand still, will ya? Assume some frozen posin' when you pass by the armor or that statue in the gallery. Who's real . . . and who's the dummy?*

Get-Your-Ghost Step IV: Put on a Good Show

Ruh-roh! Now it's my turn to tell you my own tricks for tricking terror with my pal Shaggy. You've been observant like Velma, crafty like Freddy, and have watched your step like Daphne. Now Shag and I want to PUT ON A GOOD SHOW!

Don't tell me you're scared?

Me, scared? Like, don't be silly.

Then why are you biting Scooby's nails?

Oh, so I am. . . . Sorry, Scoob.

After all, we ARE the ones who always get sent into the cave first. We're the ones already on the run when the mystery's barely begun! Have you ever noticed how Shaggy and I run? We play a game of catch up. I run fast and then Shag overtakes me and then I catch up! Sometimes there's a monster right behind us . . . but it never wins. Shaggy and I are too fast! All you'll see is its bald shadow lurking behind us.

I can't tell you the number of times I've yelped and jumped headfirst into Shaggy's arms! Like, zoinks! Sometimes I think I scare him more by doing that! But he grabs me all the same, and we take off running.

Eventually, we get pooped out or we come to a brick wall dead end.

That's when the Scooby and Shaggy Show happens.

That's when the dupe's on the demon — not the other way around!

After all, who says, "Ghouls Rule"? With a zombie on our tails, we'll try every costume, pose, and accent to confuse the beast in pursuit! Ree-hee! And we're aces at distracting creeps . . . at least for a while.

Like, a few of our better scare scams include:

- Shaggy and I played barbers to the Big Bad Werewolf. Boy, was he surprised when we tried to snip the hairs on his chinny-chin-chin!

- Grab your partner! We went west and square-danced with the green ghosts! You know, before they figured out we were tricking them into the two-step, they were having a fine time at the hoedown!

- Cowboys and Indians wins! I took on the role of Dog Star, king of the wild blue yonder, while Shaggy befuddled the ghost with his Indian song and dance. Yuk!

- Shaggy snapped his camera on that pirate ghoul when he invited him into our phony photo studio. "Say cheese! We'll mail ya the prints!" Like, sure we will.

- This one works every time: Tell a stupid bone joke . . . to a skeleton!

- Velma joined us when we duped the Tiki Witch Doctor with a little "Me Tarzan, You Jane." And I was Cheeta the chimp! We asked the voodoo king, "You look for boy, girl, dog?" and then he ran away in that direction. . . .

- We bluffed the caveman into thinking he was a guest at the thee-ahh-ter! Shaggy called for "Tickets, tickets, please!" while I took the caveman's club from him and showed him to his seat. He thought he'd be seeing a fish act! Ruffff!

- We did our best work distracting zombies at Shag and Scoob's Chinese Restaurant! How could we go wrong with a FOOD scam? After all, we claimed it was the place where ghosts eat the most — and those dead-faced monsters looked mighty hungry! Shaggy told the zombies they looked like they could stand a little fattening up so I brought along bibs for the boo boys. Our specialties of the house? Chocolate chop suey and spareribs à la mode! Yummmm!

Get-Your-Ghost Step V: Be Polite

The final step for picking up your local ghost is simple: BE POLITE. Shaggy sets an example for all of us to follow. Like, when addressing a ghoul, always call him or her *Mr.* or *Ms.* Ghoul. Or, if it's a *royal* ghoul, then call it by its proper name — whether it's King Ghoul, Princess Ghoul, or Sir Ghoul. In other words, be cool when you talk directly to a ghoul. "Like, would you *please* let go of my ear, Sir Zombie?"

Chapter 7

SECRET SCOOBY-DOO STUMPERS AND THE PAW-FECT PERSONALITY TEST

How Much Do You Know? Who Are *You* Most Like? Take This Pup Quiz Now!

What kind of sleuth are you? Are you fit to ride the Mystery Machine? Who do you resemble most in the people posse . . . or are you like me, Scooby-Doo? Take this pup quiz now . . . and find out for sure! Just go face to fur with the following questions!

T-T-TRUE OR FALSE?

First, try your paw at a few true or false questions. Are you as up on the pup as you first thought? Hmmmm? When you're done, look in the back for the answers. Give yourself one point for every correct answer. How'd you do? Rate yourself on a scale from Scoob-A to Scoob-F.

Scooby True (ST) or Scooby False (SF)

1. Scooby-Doo's real name on his pup certificate is Scoobinski. ....ST SF

2. "Ree-hee!" means: I'm so silly! ....ST SF

3. Daphne's favorite saying is "Jinkies!" ....ST SF

4. Scooby-Doo was born on Knittingham Puppy Farm..................ST SF

5. The Mystery Machine drives itself. ....ST SF

6. The gang's name is Mystery Loves Company. ....ST SF

7. Scooby Snacks come from the Scooby Snack Factory...................ST SF

8. Scooby-Doo is a great schnauzer........ST SF

9. Velma can't see without her super specs. ....ST SF

10. Scooby has blue spots on his coat......ST SF

11. "Yip! Yip! Yip!" means: "Ghoul on the loose!"......................................ST SF

12. Scooby Snacks taste like butterscotch. ....ST SF

13. Shaggy is Scooby's best buddy. ....ST SF

14. Scooby never wears disguises. ....ST SF

15. Shaggy stutters when he's freaked out. ....ST SF

16. Fred always says, "Ruh-roh!" ....ST SF

17. The bad ghouls always say, "If it weren't for those peddling kids!" as they're being dragged off. ....ST SF

M-M-M-MULTIPLE CHOICE PERSONALITY PUP QUIZ

Who are u most like? Take a look at the multiple choice part of your brain-busting Scooby exam. Like, wow. Write down your answers to each question. When you're done, add up the number of A's, B's, C's, D's, and E's. Once again, turn to the answer key in the back of the book to find out which Scooby pal you are most like.

1. *You are hungry. You open the refrigerator and pull out:*
   a) *Zoinks! A Scooby Snack!*
   b) *Fresh fruit, naturally!*
   c) *I'll take a steak. Well done.*
   d) *Like, gimme anything. I'm starvin' Marvin!*
   e) *My calculations tell me that I am not hungry right now.*

2. *It's raining and you decide to hide out at the movies. Your pick?*
   a) *Dog Ranger!* My hero!
   b) *Pretty Woman.*
   c) Action! All action!
   d) Surfin' movies only. They're outta sight!
   e) *The Nutty Professor!* My hero!

3. *You have been selected for the Laff-A-Lympics Team. What sport?*
   a) The Scooby Snack relay! Yah, yah!
   b) Ice dancing, for sure.
   c) Only a triathalon could prove my many skills.
   d) Like, foodball. I mean, football.
   e) I am not a sporty individual.

4. *Time for some music! What are your favorite tunes?*
   a) Spoooooooky-Doo music! Ree-hee!
   b) Girl groups!
   c) Whatever is the most popular, of course.
   d) Like, surfin' tunes. What else?
   e) Classical music. The obvious choice.

5. *Your friend is late for lunch in the cafeteria and you're mad. You:*
   a) Rever ret rangry!
   b) Don't care if someone is late-o! Jeepers!
   c) Be assertive. Tell them you're mad.
   d) Stay cool, man. Have a Shaggarific hero sandwich instead.
   e) The logical thing to do is to avoid conflict.

6. *What's your best excuse for not handing in your homework?*
   a) Ruh-roh. Silly me.
   b) Homework horrors! I just forgot!
   c) I'm in charge here and when I want to do homework I'll do it.
   d) It has pizza stains on it.
   e) I always do my homework.

7. *It's your best pal's birthday, and you have to get a gift. You pick out:*
   a) Ret's ret a Rooby Rack Rar! (translation: Let's get a Scooby Snack jar!)
   b) Jewelry . . . or maybe I'll just keep that for myself and get my friend something else.
   c) A dependable tie. What a good idea.
   d) Like, sneakers. Or maybe some food. Is anyone else hungry around here?
   e) The most challenging jigsaw puzzle at the puzzle store.

8. *If you could be any animal, which would you be?*
   a) Ruh-roh! Is that a trick question???
   b) Kitty cat.
   c) A dependable golden retriever.
   d) A giraffe. Yuk! Yuk! Yuk!
   e) Perhaps I would be a dolphin or ape. The most intelligent of the species, of course.

9. *How do you make a fashion statement that's all your own?*
   a) Rhinestone rog rollar!
   b) Any fashion statement I make is all my own.
   c) Any scarf will do.
   d) Like, dress a mess, man!
   e) Glasses. Big ones. Thick ones.

10. *What is your favorite color these days?*
   a) Brown?
   b) The color purple.
   c) I have so many favorites.
   d) Like, brown.
   e) Orange, like my turtleneck.

11. *You're a contestant in a dance contest.*
    What is your best step?
    a) Do-si-do. Grab yer partner! Ree-hee!
    b) All my steps are good.
    c) Real men don't dance.
    d) Like, the watusi or the twist. Far out!
    e) The polka.

12. *What was your nickname as a little kid?*
    a) The 'Doo.
    b) Belle.
    c) Know-it-all.
    d) Spazzy.
    e) Dinkley.

13. *What's in your knapsack?*
    a) Scooby Snacks and a picture of
       Mommy-Doo.
    b) Lip gloss.
    c) My spare red scarf and the keys
       to the Mystery Machine.
    d) Like, what knapsack?
    e) Compass. Map. Dictionary. Laptop
       computer. Any questions?

14. *What's your favorite after-school activity?*
    a) Chasing after ghouls. Rippppeee!
    b) Cheerleading, for sure. And hairstyling.
    c) Drivers' ed.
    d) Like, totally snoozing.
    e) I like to study after school.

15. *What book are you reading right now?*
    a) *Scooby-Doo's Guide to Life.*
       Ree-hee-hee-hee . . .
    b) Jeepers! I forget.
    c) I listen to audio books while driving.
    d) Book? Zoinks!
    e) *The Encyclopedia Britannica.*

16. *What's hidden under your bed?*
    a) Rulp. Okay. My Scooby Snack stash.
    b) Shoes, shoes, and more shoes.
    c) Nothing is under MY bed.
    d) Like, I think I saw a pizza.
    e) Back issues of *Popular Science.*

17. *Which one of the Seven Dwarfs are you
    most like?*
    a) Ruh? Rwarfs? Hmmm. Dopey?
    b) I am not a dwarf. I am Snow White.
    c) Doc. Born leader.
    d) Like, Sleepy . . . or maybe Happy.
       No! Sloppy! Yuk. Yuk.
    e) Bashful.

18. *You're thrilled to report* all *A's on your
    report card. You jump in the air and:*
    a) Clap my paws!
    b) Shake my head with disbelief. All A's? Me?
    c) Tug on my scarf. Great job, Mr. Jones!
    d) Laugh.
    e) Get back to studying immediately.

19. *On your bulletin board, you have a picture of:*
    a) Mommy-Doo and the rest of my doggy family.
    b) Fred.
    c) Daphne.
    d) A hero sandwich.
    e) Albert Einstein.

20. *Oh no! You're hungry again. This time, you reach in the fridge for:*
    a) Mesquite-grilled, chocolate-dipped, cheese-stuffed Scooby Snacks?
    b) Tofu Surprise.
    c) A six-pack of Gator Cola.
    d) Pep-pep-pepper pizza!
    e) How can you eat at a time like this?

THE ANSWERS: How You Rate

Scooby True or Scooby False Answers:
1. SF. His real name is Scoobert.
2. ST.
3. SF. Daphne doesn't say "Jinkies," Velma does.
4. ST.
5. SF. Fred drives the Mystery Machine.
6. SF. The name is Inc., Mystery, Inc.
7. ST.
8. SF. Scooby-Doo is a Great Dane.

9. ST.
10. SF. Scooby has black spots on his coat.
11. SF. "Yip! Yip! Yip!" means "Did someone say Scooby Snack?"
12. ST.
13. ST.
14. SF. Scooby *always* wears disguises.
15. ST.
16. SF. Scooby always says, "Ruh-roh!"
17. SF. The bad ghouls say, "If it weren't for those meddling kids . . ."

SCOOB-A

If you scored a perfect 17, I bow at your paws! A Scooberific success!

SCOOB-B

If you scored 13–16, take a Scooby backslap! Not too bad for a young pup like you!

SCOOB-C

If you scored 10–14, bark up! You've got a pretty good grasp of Scoob stats, but you're no Scoob expert. Time to bone up on the facts!

SCOOB-D

If you scored 5–9, head for the doghouse. Bad. Roll over. Play dead.

SCOOB-F

If you scored 4 or lower, you get a big wet dog kiss . . . and that's IT.

MULTIPLE CHOICE
PERSONALITY PUP QUIZ

Who Are U Most Like?

If You Circled Mostly A's

Say hello to Scooby-Doo! You and me (ree-hee-hee) could be as snug as two bugs in a rug! We think alike, look alike, talk alike, and even walk alike! Your love for anything Scooby Snack-ish makes you a Scoobophile of the highest order. Since you are a lot like Scooby, your strongest qualities are your chickenheartedness (who doesn't love a sensitive dog?), your laughter, and your ghoul-chasing savvy.

Congratulations on being a GREAT big DANE!

If You Circled Mostly B's

Jeepers! You even wear purple lip gloss! You've got that Daphne thing going for you . . . with good looks and everything. You might consider trading in your outfit for a new one, or maybe keeping away from trapdoors once in a while. You are ten times more likely than the average sleuth to fall into a hole in the middle of the street.

If You Circled Mostly C's

You take charge. You and Fred are like two peas in a pod. Call the shots. Make the rules. You like being boss and you're not apologizing for it. Fred-DEE! Fred-DEE! Fred-DEE!

If You Circled Mostly D's

You buzzed? Surf's up and, like, you and the Shaggmeister are like twins! Do you think this is some kind of intense coincidence or do you really believe that somewhere in the world, somewhere out there, is your twin? Like, how far out is that?! Zoinks! Wanna come over and snarf a super-duper sloppy seven-foot hero sand-wich? Yuk! Yuk!

If You Circled Mostly E's

According to our calculations, Velma and you are identical. Jinkies! Do you wear super specs, too? Scientific research shows that, just like Velma, you're destined for great-ness. You and she are on the same brainiac wavelength. Now that's smarts!

TO BARK OR NOT TO BARK

There you have it. Friends, ghoul-chasing, eating, and everything else you could possibly imagine — the Scooby-Doo way! But there's one final thing you MUST know in order to live a Great Dane life.

It's time to bark along with Scooby's Scooberific theme song! Ruh-roh!

Scooby Dooby-Doo, where are you
We got some work to do now
Scooby Dooby-Doo, where are you
We need some help from you now

C'mon, Scooby-Doo
I see you
Pretending you've got a sliver
You're not foolin' me
Cuz I can see
The way you shake and shiver

You know we got a mystery to solve
So, Scooby-Doo, be ready for your act
Don't hold back
And Scooby-Doo, if you come through
You're gonna have yourself a Scooby Snack
That's a fact

Scooby Dooby-Doo
Dooby-doo
Here are you
You're ready and you're willin'
If we can count on you
Scooby-Doo
I know we'll catch that villain.